To Emmett and Desmond.
Thanks for making our fishbowl fun.
—LP

Gouache, pencil, ink, and Photoshop were used to prepare the full color art.

Published by Sourcebooks Jabberwocky, an imprint of Sourcebooks Kids
P.O. Box 4410, Naperville, Illinois 60567-4410
(630) 961-3900
sourcebookskids.com

Library of Congress Cataloging-in-Publication Data is on file with the publisher.

Source of Production: Leo Paper, Heshan City, Guangdong Province, China
Date of Production: December 2020
Run Number: 5020166

Printed and bound in China.
LEO 10 9 8 7 6 5 4 3 2 1

TOO CROWDED

Lena Podesta

sourcebooks
jabberwocky

This is my plant.

This is my plant and my castle.

These are my pebbles.

I clean them every day.

All **138** of them.
All by myself.

This is my house.

My small, round, cramped house
with a plant, a castle,
and 138 pebbles to clean every day.

My house is TOO CROWDED!

This is my suitcase.
These are my shoes.

I will find a new house...
A house without plants or castles or pebbles.
A house that is not too crowded.

This is Bird's house.

Bird's house is not crowded
or small like my house.

Bird's house is large.
Bird's house is spacious.

This is Bird singing.

This is Bird singing loud.
All day long.

This house is TOO LOUD!

This is Cat's house.

Cat's house is not crowded like my house
or loud like Bird's house.
Cat's house is quiet.

Cat's house is **VERY** quiet.

Cat's house is
TOO DANGEROUS!

This is Turtle's house.
Turtle's house is not loud like Bird's house
or dangerous like Cat's house.

Turtle's house is...

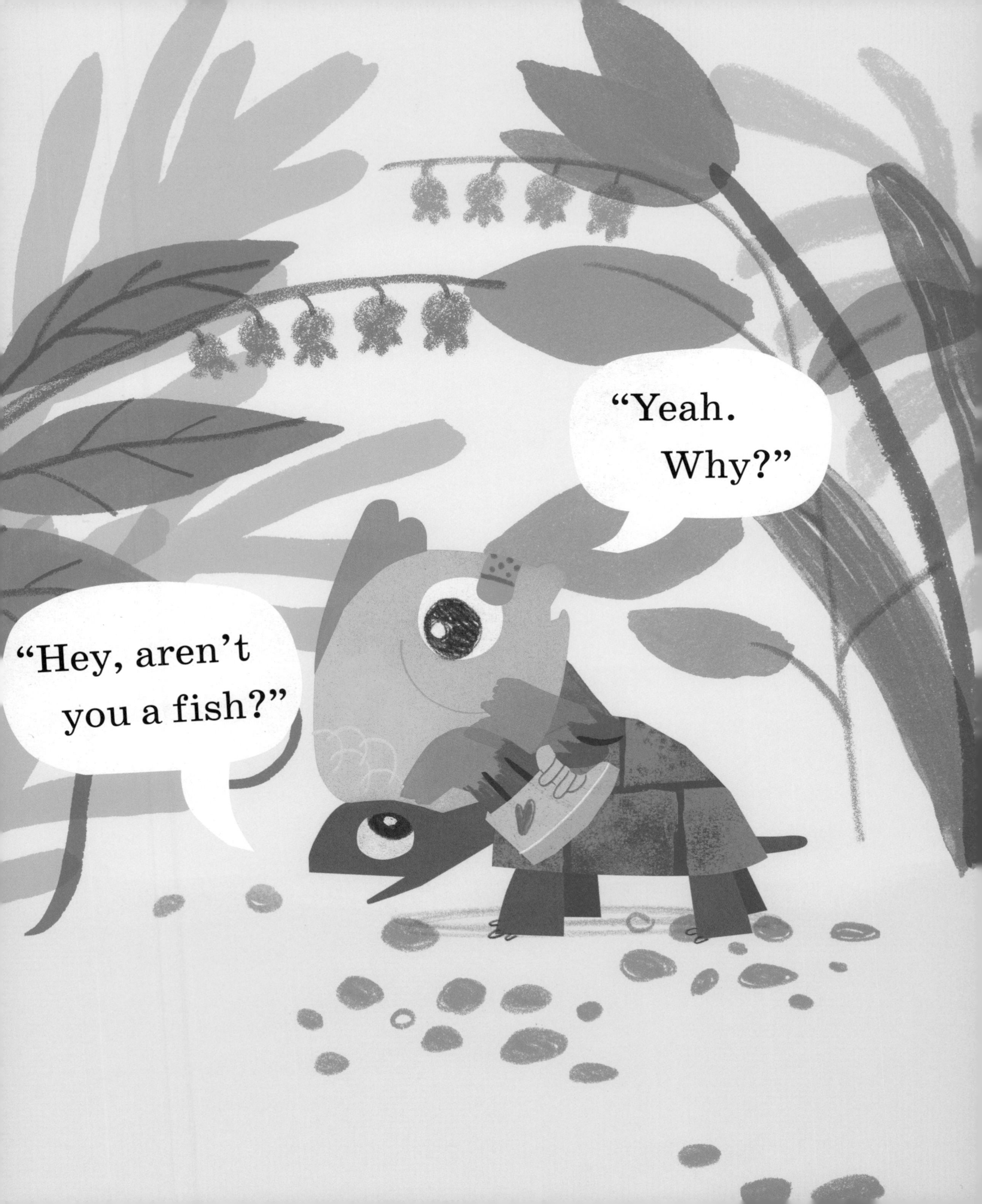
"Hey, aren't you a fish?"
"Yeah. Why?"

This is my house.

My small, round, cramped house with
138 pebbles to clean every day.

This is also Turtle's house!

This is our plant.

This is our castle.

These are our pebbles that we
clean every day...together!

Our house is not too crowded.

Our house is PERFECT.

LENA PODESTA is a professional animator and the illustrator of *Baby Dragon, Baby Dragon!* She lives with her husband and children at the bottom of a volcano in Portland, Oregon.